DATE DUE

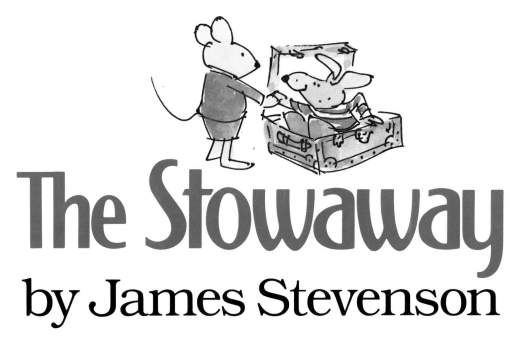

The Stowaway

by James Stevenson

Greenwillow Books, New York

Watercolor paints and a
black pen were used for
the full-color art.

Printed in Hong Kong
by South China Printing
Company (1988) Ltd.
First Edition
10 9 8 7 6 5 4 3 2 1

Library of Congress
Cataloging-in-Publication Data
Stevenson, James (date)
The stowaway.
Summary:
Hubie, a young mouse crossing
the ocean on a large cruise ship with
his parents, helps a stowaway
elude the authorities.
    [1. Mice—Fiction.
2. Ocean liners—Fiction.
3. Stowaways—Fiction.
4. Cartoons and comics]
I. Title.
PZ7.S84748St   1990
[E]   89-25861
ISBN 0-688-08619-5
ISBN 0-688-08620-9 (lib. bdg.)

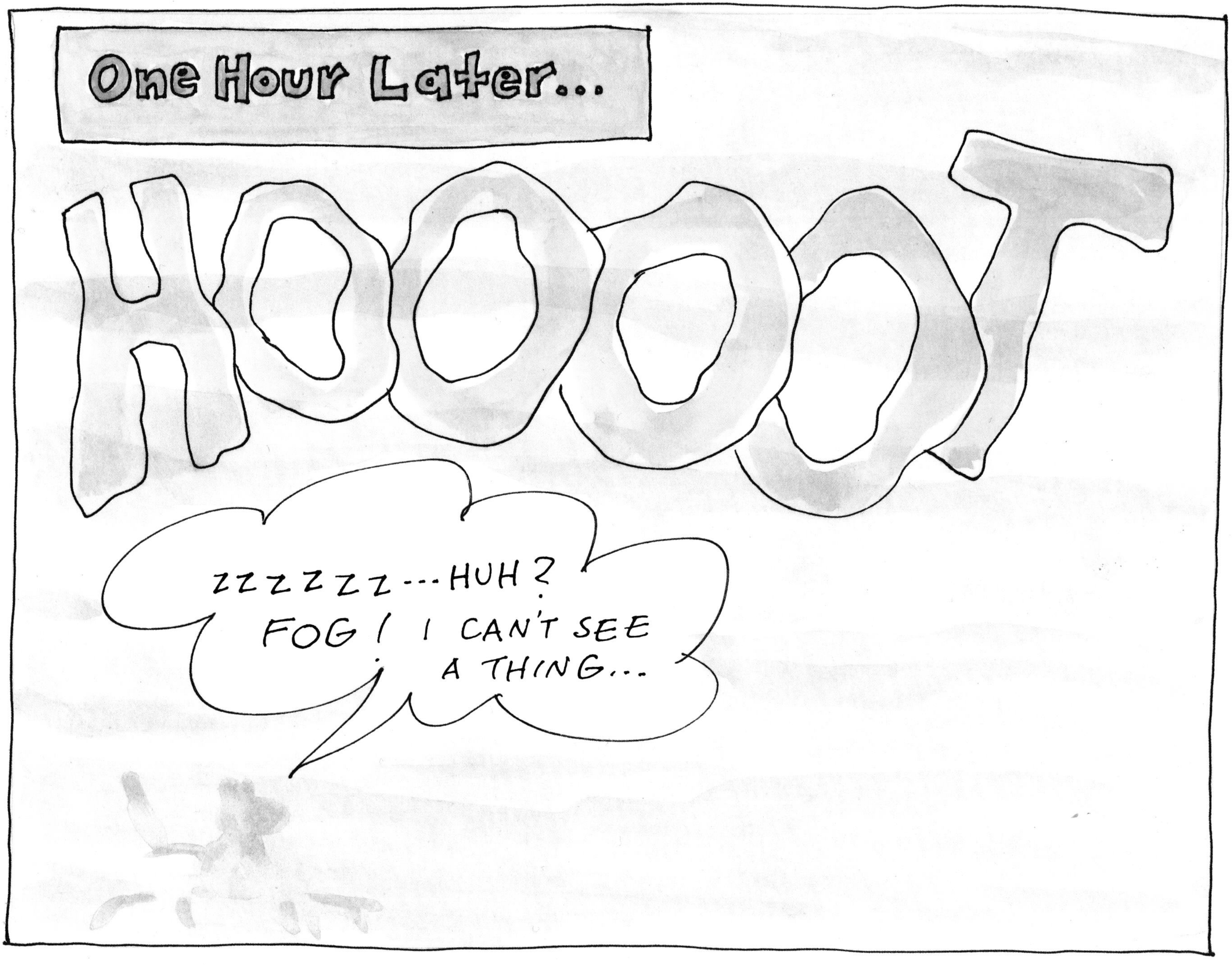
One Hour Later...
HOOOOT
ZZZZZZ...HUH? FOG! I CAN'T SEE A THING...